THE

LLOYD: A HERO'S JOURNEY

ADAPTED BY TRACEY WEST FROM THE SCREENPLAY

STORY BY HILARY WINSTON & BOB LOGAN & PAUL FISHER AND
BOB LOGAN & PAUL FISHER & WILLIAM WHEELER & TOM WHEELER

SCREENPLAY BY BOB LOGAN & PAUL FISHER & WILLIAM WHEELER
& TOM WHEELER AND JARED STERN & JOHN WHITTINGTON

SCHOLASTIC INC.

Adapted by Tracey West from the screenplay

Story by Hilary Winston & Bob Logan & Paul Fisher and Bob Logan &
Paul Fisher & William Wheeler & Tom Wheeler

Screenplay by Bob Logan & Paul Fisher & William Wheeler &
Tom Wheeler and Jared Stern & John Whittington

All rights reserved. Published by Scholastic Inc., *Publishers since 1920*. SCHOLASTIC
and associated logos are trademarks and/or registered trademarks of Scholastic Inc.

ISBN 978-1-338-13966-2

10 9 8 7 6 5 4 3 2 1   17 18 19 20 21

Printed in the U.S.A.   40

First printing 2017
Book design by Jessica Meltzer

Hey there! I'm Lloyd, and I'm the Green Ninja. I live in Ninjago City.

I love building high-tech mechs. Mechs are giant robots with pilots inside. Mine is a Mech Dragon. When I'm in my mech, I can fly!

I build mechs for the other members of my ninja team, too.

There are six of us, and we're the Secret Ninja Force. Each one of us brings a different skill to the team.

This is Kai. He's got a lot of energy. He never backs down from a challenge.

Nya is Kai's sister. She's really brave and takes her ninja training seriously.

Jay is almost never serious. He's always joking around. But he's a great inventor and a skilled ninja. He gets serious when we're in battle.

Cole stays cool and calm when things get crazy. He's also strong and tough to take down.

Zane might be a Nindroid, but he's got a good heart inside that mechanical body. He helps keep us all focused.

Like all ninjas, we've got a master—a teacher. His name is Master Wu. Don't be fooled by his long, white beard. He's a fierce fighter. He's tough on us, but that's okay. Because we've got lots of bad guys to deal with.

Lord Garmadon is the baddest bad guy of them all. He's got red eyes, sharp teeth, and four arms! He also rides around in a giant robot shark—his shark mech called the Garma Mecha Man.

One day, Lord Garmadon stomped into Ninjago City in his Garma Mecha Man. Citizens ran and screamed as he started blasting everything in sight. He laughed at them from his perch on top of the shark mech.

One poor guy tripped and fell. Lord Garmadon was about to step on him. But I swooped in on my Mech Dragon. I grabbed the guy before he got squashed.

"Thanks, Green Ninja!" he said.

Then Jay flew up next to us in his mech.

"Lloyd, that was my save," he said over the comm link.

"Jay, you can't save him," I told him. "He's already saved."

"Well, drop him, and then I'll save him," Jay said.

I didn't have time to argue with Jay. I let him save the guy. Then I flew off.

I passed Kai in his Fire Mech. He was blasting flames at Lord Garmadon's army of Piranha Mechs and Flying Mantas.

"I'm going after Garmadon," I said.

Then . . . *boom!* A blast from the shark mech hit me.

It knocked me off my Mech Dragon. I flew through the air . . . and right into a gang of scary Sharkmen!

The Sharkmen chased me into a room. A baby was crying in his crib. I picked up the baby, but I had to keep fighting the Sharkmen.

Out in the street, Zane entered the battle. He shot freezing blasts at enemy mechs from the barrels of his Ice Tank.

"Where's Lloyd?" he asked into the comm link.

"In the kitchen," I replied.

Bam! I took down the last Sharkman with a refrigerator door. Then I gave the baby back to his mom.

Outside, the other ninja were battling Lord Garmadon's mechanical army. Cole rolled through the city on the single, giant wheel of his Quake Mech. He slammed his big metal fists into the ground.

Whomp! The shock wave sent five of Garmadon's army flying backward.

More mechanical sharks swarmed in from the harbor.

"This is getting serious," Cole said.

He spun a record on his control panel. Loud, intense music blasted from the Quake Mech's massive speakers. The sound shattered the enemy mechs into pieces!

Windows on the buildings shattered, too! One citizen nearly fell out of a broken window, but her co-worker caught her by the arm. She dangled high above the city.

Then . . . *whoosh!* Nya zoomed up in her Water Strider and rescued her.

I got back in my Dragon Mech and flew straight for Lord Garmadon. I didn't wait for my teammates.

"Well, hello, Green Ninja!" Lord Garmadon said. "You ready for me to conquer Ninjago City today?"

"I don't think so," I replied. "Your mechs are no match for our high-tech mechs!"

Lord Garmadon knew I was right. "I'll be back!" he promised. "And when I do, I'll have something really wicked for you!"

"Oh, I'll be waiting for you," I said. Then I added softly, "Dad . . ."

"What did you say?" Garmadon asked.

You see, Lord Garmadon is my dad.

"I'll be waiting," I repeated. "Dad . . ."

I said it softly again, so he couldn't hear me. He shrugged and called to his army.

"Come, let us return to my volcanic lair!" Then he gave an evil laugh. "For now."

We had saved Ninjago City! The Secret Ninja Force headed back to *Destiny's Bounty*. It's an old ship, and our secret training dojo.

We were all cheering when we saw Master Wu. But he was frowning.

"You keep blowing things up with your crazy machines," he said. "Garmadon will be back. So you have won nothing."

"What do you want us to do?" Cole asked.

Master Wu brought us to the dojo, our training room. He made us all sit on the floor and close our eyes.

"I want you to let the mellow sounds of nature guide you on the path to inner balance," Master Wu replied.

I tried to find my inner balance. But all I could see when I closed my eyes was the face of Lord Garmadon. My dad. His red eyes flashed angrily. It upset me. It was hard having Ninjago's greatest villain as my dad!

"I just want to have a normal life!" I told Master Wu. "I just want this to end."

Master Wu sighed. "Lloyd, you are winning the battle on the outside," he said. "But you are losing the battle on the inside."

I wasn't exactly sure what Master Wu meant. But at that moment, I knew one thing.

Somehow, I had to find my inner balance. I would learn to become the best ninja ever.

And I would stop my father, Lord Garmadon, once and for all!

Copyright © 2017 Warner Bros. Entertainment Inc. & The LEGO Group.
THE LEGO NINJAGO MOVIE © & ™ Warner Bros. Entertainment Inc. & The LEGO Group. LEGO, the LEGO logo, the Minifigure, the Brick and Knob configurations and NINJAGO are trademarks and/or copyrights of the LEGO Group. © 2017 The LEGO Group. All rights reserved. (s17)
ISBN: 978-1-338-13966-2
PO# 564768